FIONA THE PIG

Leigh HOBBS

Running Press
KIDS
PHILADELPHIA·LONDON

For Julie Watts

Printed in China

This book may not be reproduced in whole or in part, in any form or by any means, electronic or mechanical, including photocopying, recording, or by any information storage and retrieval system now known or hereafter invented, without written permission from the publisher.

9   8   7   6   5   4   3   2   1

Digit on the right indicates the number of this printing

Library of Congress Control Number: 2004100220
ISBN 0-7624-2092-8
Originally published in Australia by Penguin Books Australia, Ltd
Original design by Leigh Hobbs and Marina Messiha, Penguin Design Studio.
Additional design for this edition by Frances Soo Ping Chow

Typography: Bembo

This book may be ordered by mail from the publisher.
Please include $2.50 for postage and handling.
But try your bookstore first!

This edition published by Running Press Kids,
an imprint of
Running Press Book Publishers
125 South Twenty-second Street
Philadelphia, Pennsylvania 19103-4399

Visit us on the web!
www.runningpress.com

Fiona was a pig.
Her bedroom was neat and pretty, just like Fiona.

She lived with her parents in Pig Towers.
Fiona adored her parents and they adored her.

But Mr. and Mrs. Pig were baffled.
Their daughter wasn't a bit like them.

For example: every day, Fiona preened and pampered herself in her perfumed bubble bath. Fiona even had a collection of scented soaps!

"What's soap?" Mrs. Pig would ask. "Why can't she wallow in mud like we do?"

Fiona had no idea her parents were worried.

She was always busy making herself nice—doing her nails, putting her hair up and powdering her nose.

In the mornings Fiona liked to join her parents and watch cartoons. But only after she had brushed her teeth, dressed her dollies and tidied her room.

"What a little fusspot!" Mr. Pig would sigh.

Fiona often had her dollies around for afternoon tea.

She liked to serve little cakes with pink icing and fancy chocolate cookies.

"*I've* never heard of a pig serving dainty cakes from
a silver tray," Mrs. Pig would always say. "Why won't
Fiona use a wheelbarrow like I taught her to?"

"What's wrong with that little pig?" Fiona's father would ask in between burps. "We brought her up so carefully."

"Indeed we did," Mrs. Pig would reply. "She's becoming a real problem. Why can't she be more like . . . US?"

One day Fiona noticed that her parents looked a bit glum.
So she decided to give them a treat.

First she cut out some fairy wings.

Then she made a fairy dress.

Then she ironed
her costume carefully.

Then she practiced singing.

After that, she taught herself to tap dance.

The next day, Fiona handed out some special invitations.
Then she had a quick rest.

Fiona had to save her strength, for soon
she would be very busy.

There were curtains to hang, wings to put on,
hair to put up, tap shoes to strap tight . . .

. . . and two very special pigs to guide to their seats.

Fiona was putting on a little show,

for her parents . . .

. . . and the pig downstairs.

Fiona performed her ballet, "Pigs Can Fly."

She loved her parents very much and so she danced and tapped . . .

. . . and sang with all her heart.

After her final song, Mr. and Mrs. Pig clapped politely, smiled and left the room.

But that night they lay awake thinking and worrying.

"Why can't our daughter be more like a pig?" whispered Fiona's father.

"Yes," agreed Fiona's mother. "She should be more like *us*!"

In the morning Mr. and Mrs. Pig visited Dr. Pinkysnout and explained their problem.

"There doesn't seem to *be* a problem," said the doctor. "Fiona sounds *adorable*. Most pigs are very clean and very neat, you know."

Now Mr. and Mrs. Pig were *completely* confused. "Maybe we need to be more like Fiona," they said to themselves as they rushed home.

"I'll clean the house," said Mrs. Pig as soon as she arrived. "Fiona will like that."

But housework was far too hard and anyway, Mrs. Pig liked the way her home looked!

"I'll learn to tap dance," said Mr. Pig.
"It will be good for my health."

But, it wasn't good for anyone else's.
Pig Towers shook and swayed . . .

. . . and the pig downstairs was furious.

Meanwhile, Fiona was preparing tea and cake for her dollies . . .

. . . and two extra special guests, who had realized something *very* important—

Their daughter would *never* be like them, *that's* for sure. But Mr. and Mrs. Pig adored Fiona, no matter what.

As for Fiona, of *course* she adored *them*.
She didn't care that her parents were pigs.

After all . . .

Fiona was a pig, too.